Curious George®

GOES TO THE AQUARIUM

Adapted from the Curious George film series

Edited by Margret Rey and Alan J. Shalleck

1 9 8 4
Houghton Mifflin Company Boston

Library of Congress Cataloging in Publication Data
Main entry under title:

Curious George goes to the aquarium.

"Adapted from the Curious George film series."
Summary: Curious George jumps in with the seals
during his visit to the aquarium and becomes the star
attraction.
1. Children's stories, American. [1. Aquariums—Fic-
tion. 2. Monkeys—Fiction] I. Rey, Margret.
II. Shalleck, Alan J. III. Curious George goes to the
aquarium (Motion picture)
PZ7.C9217   1984   [E]   84-16828
ISBN 0-395-36634-8 (lib. bdg.)
ISBN 0-395-36628-3 (pbk.)

Printed in Japan

10 9 8 7 6 5 4 3 2 1

"Let's go to the aquarium today, George,"
said the man with the yellow hat.

The manager of the aquarium met them at the door.
"I'm going to feed the seals now," he said.
"Would you like to come and watch?"

He took a pail full of fish, went to the seal tank,
and held up one. Billy, the big seal, jumped
straight into the air and caught it.

George was fascinated.

Next, Billy did a twist in the air.

George liked the seals,
but only a few people were watching.

"The next show will be at two P.M.," announced the manager.

George went behind the fish tanks. There was a net
on a long pole leaning against a tank.

George was curious. Could he feed the seals, too?

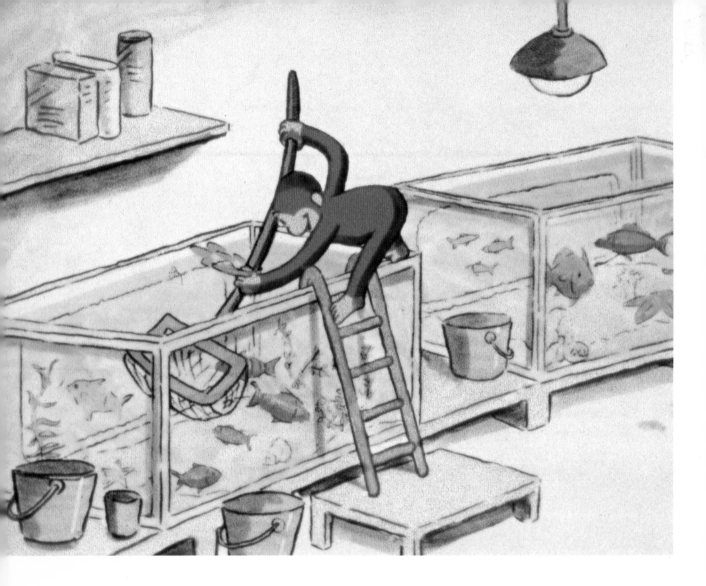

He took the net, went to the tank, and dipped it
into the water.

George caught lots of fish!

Just then, a guard came by and saw the net in the tank.
"What's going on?" he shouted.

He blew his whistle.

Guards came running from all sides. "There he is,"
cried one. "Somebody catch that monkey!"

"Stop him!" shouted another.
They all ran after George.

George was scared. He ran away

and headed for the seal tank.
Meanwhile, the next show had started.

George jumped right into the tank and
landed on the back of a seal.

"Look, a monkey!" someone shouted.

One seal flipped George high into the air.

Another seal caught him.

All the seals poked their heads out of the water.
They all wanted to play with George.

They tossed George into the air and
took turns catching him.

George was having lots of fun.

The audience went wild.
It was the best show they had ever seen.

Finally, George landed on the platform.

Suddenly, a guard reached out and grabbed him by the ear.

The manager rushed over. "Wait," he said.
"Let George go! He was the star of the show."

"Can we hire George?" the manager asked.
"We'll see," said the man in the yellow hat,
"but I think I'd better take him home now."

They all cheered George once more.